To Our darling Ailsa

From Nana Pa-ga Feb 2021

MR. MEN™ LITTLE MISS™ © THOIP (a SANRIO company)

Mr. Men Little Miss My Mummy © 2017 THOIP (a SANRIO company)
Printed and published under licence from Penguin Random House LLC
This edition published in Great Britain 2021 by Egmont Books

An imprint of HarperCollins*Publishers*
1 London Bridge Street, London SE1 9GF

www.egmontbooks.co.uk

ISBN 978 1 4052 9964 0
66494/001
Printed in Italy

Stay safe online. Egmont is not responsible for content hosted by third parties.

Egmont takes its responsibility to the planet and its inhabitants very seriously.
We aim to use papers from well-managed forests run by responsible suppliers.

MY MUMMY

by Roger Hargreaves

and me

My mummy brightens my day from the moment she wakes up.

She is like Little Miss Sunshine on a cloudy day.

My mummy can do more than one thing at a time, like magic.

And when she reads
me stories, I feel like
I'm really there.

My mummy is very friendly and likes to talk a lot.

But she is also very good at listening, especially to me.

My mummy is very curious and sometimes asks lots of questions.

But she is also very wise and knows lots of answers.

My mummy knows when I am hungry.

And when I am tired.

My mummy can be very silly and always makes me smile.

She gives the best hugs
and knows just when they
are needed.

My mummy has a splendid sense of style.

And she has lots of interesting things stored in mysterious boxes.

My mummy loves eating cake, just like me.

And sometimes she needs time to herself, too.

My mummy can be a bit cheeky.

But she is always kind.

My mummy is lots of fun
and loves birthday parties.

She is really good at playing
games like hide-and-seek.

And my mummy is a brilliant dancer, too.

Even when things go wrong, my mummy makes me smile.

When she giggles, it makes me giggle too.

And when I make my mummy happy, she jumps for joy!

There is no one like my mummy, though sometimes I wish there were two of her.

My mummy is SO very special. My mummy loves me,
and I love my mummy.

MY MUMMY

My mummy is most like **LITTLE MISS**...

I love it when my mummy reads ....

.... to me.

My mummy makes me laugh when...

....

She always knows when...

....

My mummy is very kind because ....

....

My mummy is lots of fun and likes ....

Her favourite game to play with me is ....

I know she loves me when ....

My mummy's hugs are the best because ....

....

This is a picture
of my mummy:

by ....

aged ....